RUDOLPH

THE
RED-NOSED REINDEER

Rudolph Saves the Day

SQUARE FISH

An Imprint of Macmillan
175 Fifth Avenue, New York, NY 10010
mackids.com

RUDOLPH THE RED-NOSED REINDEER®: RUDOLPH SAVES THE DAY.
Rudolph the Red-Nosed Reindeer © & ® or TM The Rudolph Co., L.P.
All elements under license to Character Arts, LLC. All rights reserved.
Printed in China by RR Donnelley Asia Printing Solutions Ltd.,
Dongguan City, Guangdong Province.

Square Fish and the Square Fish logo are trademarks of Macmillan

Square Fish books may be purchased for business or promotional use.
For information on bulk purchases, please contact the
Macmillan Corporate and Premium Sales Department at
(800) 221-7945 x5442 or by e-mail at specialmarkets@macmillan.com.

First Square Fish Edition: 2014
Book designed by Kathleen Breitenfeld
Square Fish logo designed by Filomena Tuosto

ISBN 978-1-250-05049-6
10 9 8 7 6 5 4 3 2

Welcome to the North Pole! In a special place called Christmastown lives Santa Claus, Mrs. Claus, the elves, and the reindeer.

One day, a reindeer named Rudolph was born. Right away, his tiny red nose began to glow!

Rudolph's parents were surprised.
So was Santa.

Rudolph's father wanted Rudolph to be on the sleigh team, so he hid Rudolph's shining, red nose.

Rudolph didn't like his nose being covered. It looked funny.

Not long after, a young doe named Clarice told Rudolph he was cute!

When Rudolph heard that, he was so happy, he flew right into the air!
But then his nose cover fell off.

The other reindeer laughed and teased. They wouldn't let Rudolph join in any reindeer games.

Rudolph felt like a misfit.

Soon, Rudolph met another misfit, Hermey the Elf.

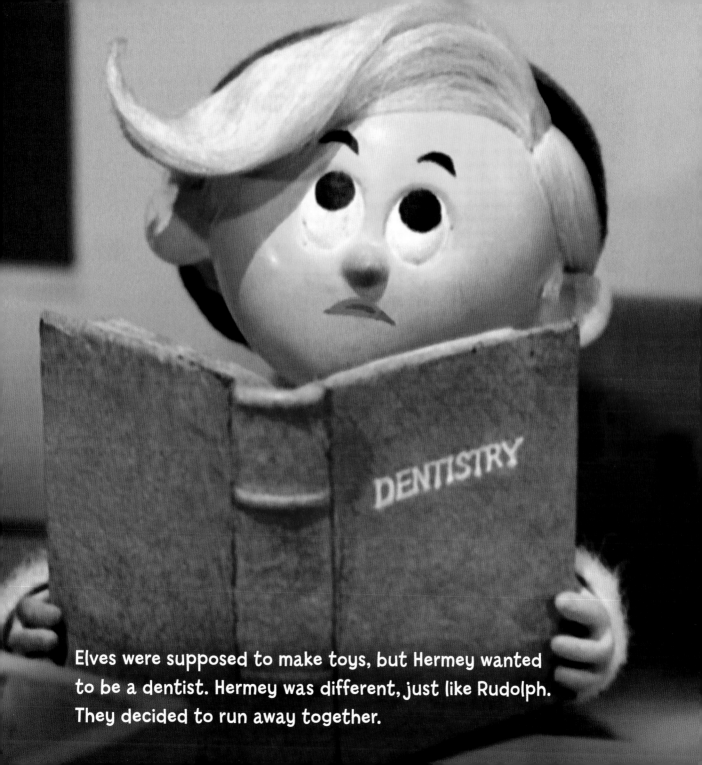

Elves were supposed to make toys, but Hermey wanted to be a dentist. Hermey was different, just like Rudolph. They decided to run away together.

Along the way, they met another friend, Yukon Cornelius. But soon, they were being chased by the Abominable Snow Monster!

Even from far away,
the monster could
see Rudolph's
bright red nose.

Rudolph didn't want to put his new friends in danger, so he bravely set out on his own.

But the Abominable Snow Monster chased him everywhere!
Rudolph decided to go home.

When he arrived home, a big storm was on the way and his parents and Clarice were gone! Rudolph knew just where to look for his family. Sure enough, he found them in the cave of the Abominable Snow Monster.

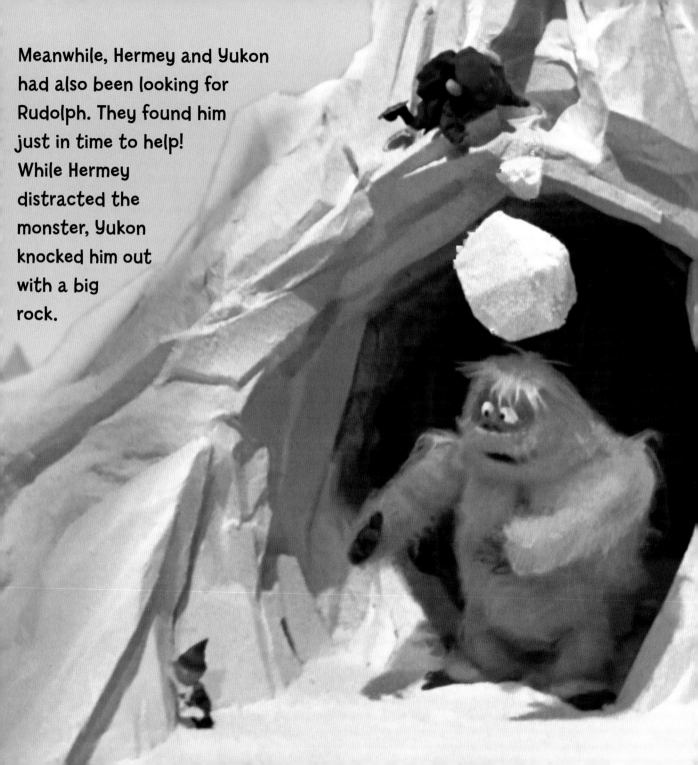

Meanwhile, Hermey and Yukon had also been looking for Rudolph. They found him just in time to help! While Hermey distracted the monster, Yukon knocked him out with a big rock.

Hermey removed all of the monster's teeth.
Finally, he got to be a dentist!

Without his teeth, the Abominable Snow Monster became friendly. He even placed the star on top of the Christmas tree! Everyone cheered!

But that night, the storm got so bad that Santa said they would have to cancel Christmas. Until . . . he had an idea.

"Rudolph," said Santa, "with your nose so bright, won't you guide my sleigh tonight?"

With Rudolph and his bright nose in the lead, Christmas was saved! And Rudolph went down in history as the greatest reindeer ever!